A Note to Parents and Teachers

Dorling Kindersley Readers is a compelling new program for beginning readers, designed in conjunction with leading literacy experts, including Dr. Linda Gambrell, Director of the School of Education at Clemson University. Dr. Gambrell has served on the Board of Directors of the International Reading Association and as President of the National Reading Conference.

Beautiful illustrations and superb full-color photographs combine with engaging, easy-to-read stories to offer a fresh approach to each subject in the series. Each *Dorling Kindersley Reader* is guaranteed to capture a child's interest while developing his or her reading skills, general knowledge, and love of reading.

The four levels of *Dorling Kindersley Readers* are aimed at different reading abilities, enabling you to choose the books that are exactly right for your child:

Level 1 – Beginning to read
Level 2 – Beginning to read alone
Level 3 – Reading alone
Level 4 – Proficient readers

The "normal" age at which a child begins to read can be anywhere from three to eight years old, so these levels are only a general guideline.

No matter which level you select, you can be sure that you are helping your child learn to read, then read to learn!

Dorling DK Kindersley

LONDON, NEW YORK, SYDNEY, DELHI, PARIS,
MUNICH, and JOHANNESBURG

Project Editor Caryn Jenner
Art Editor Jane Horne
Senior Art Editor Clare Shedden
Managing Editor Bridget Gibbs
Senior DTP Designer Bridget Roseberry
US Editor Regina Kahney
Production Shivani Pandey
Picture Researcher Angela Anderson
Jacket Designer Yumiko Tahata
Natural History Consultant
Theresa Greenaway

Reading Consultant
Linda Gambrell, Ph.D.

First American Edition, 2001
00 01 02 03 04 05 10 9 8 7 6 5 4 3 2 1
Published in the United States by DK Publishing, Inc.
95 Madison Avenue, New York, New York 10016

Published in Great Britain by Dorling Kindersley Limited.

ISBN 0-7894-7355-0 (pbk) ISBN 0-7894-7356-9 (plc)

The publisher would like to thank the following for their kind
permission to reproduce their photographs:
Position key: c=center; b=bottom; l=left; r=right; t=top

Bruce Coleman Ltd: Jeff Foott 16-17; N.H.P.A.: 22-23, 25b;
Gerrard Lacz 2c, 6-7, 15, 28t, 32bl; Kevin Schafer 2b, 24;
Planet Earth Pictures: Ken Lucas 8-9, 32bl, 33; Telegraph Colour
Library: 4-5, 5b; David Fleetham 26-27, 29t; David Nardina 2t, 9tr;
Doug Perrine 18, 19, 20, 28b, 31, 32tr; Gnadinger 14b, 21t;
John Seagrim 29b; Masterfile 30; Peter Scoones 12-13;
Planet Earth/James D Watt 25c, 32cr2; S. Hilary 23 inset, 32cr1;
Steve Bloom 10-11, 19.

Color reproduction by Colourscan, Singapore
Printed and bound in China by L. Rex Printing Co., Ltd.

see our complete
catalog at
www.dk.com

DORLING KINDERSLEY *READERS*

BEGINNING **1** *TO READ*

Diving
Dolphin

Written by Karen Wallace

DK

A Dorling Kindersley Book

A young dolphin
dives through the water.
His shiny skin is
as smooth as satin.
Far below,
he sees his mother.

His baby sister
swims beside her mother.

flipper

The young dolphin twirls
beside his mother.
Their flippers touch.
They rub each other's beaks.

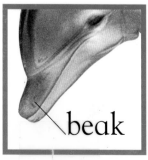
beak

Where has the
baby dolphin gone?

Mother dolphin calls her baby.
She makes a special
whistling sound.

Whistle!
Whistle!

The baby hears her mother calling.
The baby turns and
stays beside her.

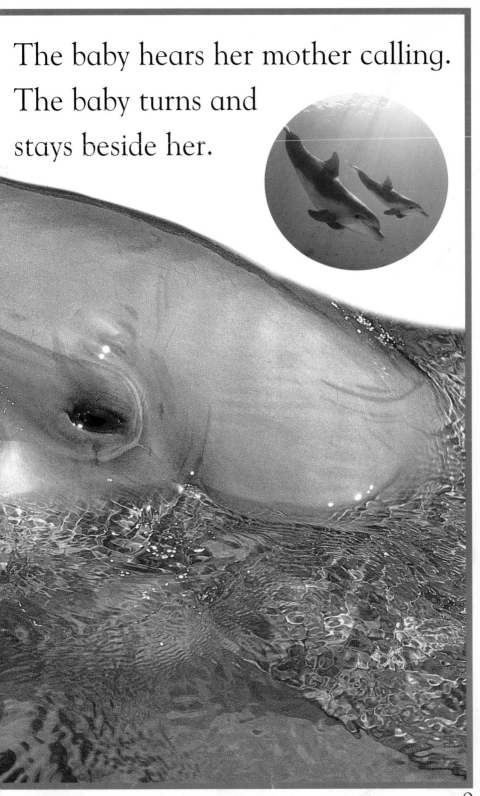

The young dolphin swims away
with older dolphins.
He leaves his mother
and his baby sister.

tail

He twirls and leaps
with the older dolphins.
They splash the water
with their tails.

Hundreds of fish
flash through the water.
The fish turn together.

They squeal and whistle.
When one swims off
the others follow.

The young dolphin
roams the ocean.
He hunts for fish
through beds of seaweed.

He rides the waves
to travel faster.
The waves push him
over the sparkling water.

waves

The dolphin leaps
as the sun is setting.
The sea is smooth
and fish are hiding.

The dolphin sees the fish
in the water.
They glow like stars
far beneath him.

The dolphin chases
the fish.
He swims down and down
to the sandy seabed.

killer
whale

He does not know
that killer whales
watch him from above.
The killer whales are hungry.

The killer whales
shoot through the water.
Their jaws are strong.
Their teeth are like knives.

jaw

The young dolphin
gives a warning whistle.
The other dolphins
race away.

The killer whales
swim through the water.
The dolphins hear them
coming closer.

The young dolphin hides.
He makes no sound.
This time the killer whales
don't find him.

The dolphin leaps.
He breathes in air
through a blowhole
on the top of
his head.

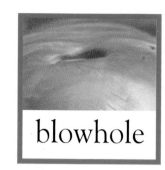

blowhole

The dolphin dives again.
A turtle watches him.

An octopus waggles past
through the water.

Now the young dolphin
swims back to his mother.
His baby sister
has grown bigger.
Their flippers touch.
They rub each other's beaks.

Soon the dolphin
will hunt for fish again.

Picture word list

flipper

page 6

waves

page 19

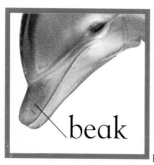

beak

page 7

killer whale

page 23

tail

page 11

jaw

page 25

teeth

page 14

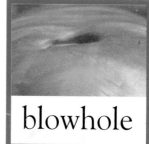

blowhole

page 28